W9-DAQ-803

The Girl Who Wouldn't Get Married

by Ruth Belov Gross

pictures by Jack Kent

FOUR WINDS PRESS
New York

Based on the Norwegian story "The Squire's Bride" by P. C. Asbjornsen.

 Published by Four Winds Press, A Division of Scholastic Inc., 730 Broadway, New York, N.Y. 10003.
Manufactured in the United States of America

10 9 8 7 6 5 4 3 2 1

The text of this book is set in 16 pt. Garamond Book.
The illustrations are full-color ink and watercolor drawings.

Library of Congress Cataloging in Publication Data
Gross, Ruth Belov. The girl who wouldn't get married.
"Based on the Norwegian story, The squire's bride, from Fairy tales from the far north, by P. C. Asbjornsen"
Summary: A rich farmer who tries to trick his neighbor's daughter into marrying him finds the unwilling girl can match him trick for trick.
[1. Folklore — Norway. 2. Marriage — Fiction]
I. Kent, Jack, 1920- ill. II. Asbjornsen, Peter Christen, 1812–1885. Herremannsbruden. III. Title.
PZ8.1.G894Gi 1983 398.2′2′09481 [E] 83-1458
ISBN 0-590-07908-5

Any girl
would be lucky
to have me.

There was once a farmer who was very rich.
He had a big farm
and lots of money in the bank.
The rich farmer did not have a wife.
But he was sure he could easily get one.

One day the farmer was walking in his hayfield.
He saw his neighbor's daughter there, hard at work.
The farmer liked the girl right away
and decided to marry her.

After a while the farmer could see
that the girl did not want to marry him.

The farmer thought he might have better luck
if he talked to the girl's father.
The girl's father said, "Leave it to me.
I will see that she marries you.
I promise."

But he could not talk his daughter into marrying the rich farmer.

The rich farmer got tired of waiting for his bride.
He sent for the girl's father and said,
"You promised me your daughter.
You must keep your promise NOW!"

I have an idea....

The girl's father said, "My daughter
has a mind of her own
and will not listen to me."
Still and all, a promise was a promise.
He had to think of something.
At last he said,
"There is only one thing left to do.

"Get everything ready for the wedding," he said.
"Then send for my daughter.
She will think you want her to do some work.
But as soon as she gets to the house — marry her!
Don't give her a chance to say no."

The rich farmer liked the idea very much.
So the next day
everyone at his house got busy.

They baked the wedding cake.

They sewed the wedding dress.

They made the wedding veil.

They invited the wedding guests.

They cooked the wedding dinner.

They cut the wedding flowers.

They cleaned every part of the house.

Then they sent for the parson.

When everything was ready,
it was time to get the bride.
"Quick!" the farmer shouted to a boy.
"Run to my neighbor! Tell him to send
what he promised me. Hurry!"

"My master wants what you promised him —
right now!" the boy said.
"Oh, yes," the girl's father said.
"She is down in the meadow.
Just run over and take her."

"Good morning, miss," the boy said.
"I have come to get what your father
promised my master."
The girl guessed what the men were up to.
"Let me think," she said. "Oh, yes!
My father promised that little bay mare of ours.
Just run over and take her."

The boy jumped on the little bay mare.
Then he rode back to the rich farmer's house
as fast as he could.

"Did you bring her with you?" the farmer asked.

"Yes, sir," said the boy. "She is right at the door."

"Good," said the farmer. "Now take her upstairs."

"Upstairs, master?" said the boy. "Upstairs?
I am sure I could never get her up those stairs."

"Just do what I say!" said the farmer.

"And be quick about it!"

Ooooh!
Ow!
Ugh!

C'mon, horse!
Uhhh!

"Well, she's upstairs at last, master,"
the boy said. "It was a terrible job —
the worst job I ever had to do on this farm."
"What a lazy boy!" the farmer said. "Always grumbling!
Now send the women up to dress her."

"But master —" said the boy.

"What's got into you?" the farmer said.

"Get a move on! And tell the women
they must not forget the bride's crown
or her flowers."

The boy ran into the kitchen
and told the women what they had to do.

The women didn't know where to begin.
They had never dressed a horse before.

They did their very best.
They put the veil and the train
and the wedding dress on the little bay mare.
They did not forget the crown or the flowers.

At last the little bay mare was dressed.

She is all ready now, master," the boy said.

"Good," the rich farmer said.

"Bring her down to me!

The guests are waiting!"

There was a loud clatter on the stairs.

The farmer turned around.

He opened his mouth.

"Aaaggggghhhhhh!" he said. "Oh! Oh, no! No!"

The guests looked at the rich farmer
and at the little bay mare.
They all burst out laughing.

Even the parson had to laugh.

The rich farmer didn't think it was funny at all.
He did not get married that day.
And he never tried to get married again.